MY BEIJING

FOUR STORIES OF EVERYDAY WONDER

NIE JUN

Translated by EDWARD GAUVIN

Graphic Universe™ • Minneapolis

THANKS TO MR. WANGNING, MANAGING DIRECTOR OF BEIJING TOTAL VISION, NICOLAS GRIVEL, AND MY WIFE, GE JING
—NIE JUN

Story and illustrations by Nie Jun
Translation by Edward Gauvin

First American edition published in 2018 by Graphic Universe™

Graphic Universe™
A division of Lerner Publishing Group, Inc.
241 First Avenue North
Minneapolis, MN 55401 USA

For reading levels and more information, look up this title at www.lernerbooks.com.

Photo on page 123: Rolf_52/Getty Images.
Title font: Anastasia Sergeeva/Shutterstock.com.

Main body text set in Andy Std 11/11.5. Typeface provided by Monotype Typography.

Library of Congress Cataloging-in-Publication Data

The Cataloging-in-Publication Data for My Beijing: Four Stories of Everyday Wonder is on file at the Library of Congress.
ISBN 978-1-5124-4590-9 (lib. bdg.)
ISBN 978-1-5415-2642-6 (pbk.)
ISBN 978-1-5124-9859-2 (eb pdf)

LC record available at https://lccn.loc.gov/2017055276

Manufactured in the United States of America
1-42520-26196-2/6/2018

YU'ER'S DREAM

Professional swimmers are like classically trained dancers. Their dives off the starting block look like ballet moves. They make graceful curves with their bodies...

* Yu: fish; er: child

She's hanging from a tree... to learn to swim! Cool idea!

So, you like the pool? I made it especially for my little champion.

Of course!

I love you, Grampa!

Oh man!

That looks hard! Kinda like being on a leash.

It's serious stuff. I heard she's training for the Olympics...

9

Whenever Yu'er's grandpa reached the middle of their neighborhood bridge, pedaling hard, he'd lift up his bottom and let out a giant toot. After that, the tricycle went as fast as lightning!

On days like these, Yu'er loved falling asleep on her grandpa's back. It felt like the belly of a bear, soft and warm.

Day after day, she didn't let doubts keep her from practicing...

I'm swimming now!

Look, is that...it's Yu'er!

Awesome! Let's follow her!

Grampa was right. When we believe in ourselves, we make our own luck...

THE END

BUG
PARADISE

In the summer, the old hutong was just swarming with insects ... *

* *hutong*: a narrow lane or alley formed by lines of courtyard homes. Among the many cities in China, Beijing is best known for its hutongs.

Well, well! A pretty little unexpected visitor…

28

His wings are damaged. The other butterflies'll make fun of him.

Put him in the jar. He'll be safe there.

But he can't fly anymore!

And he didn't do anything wrong...

I've got an idea! I know a place that could save him!

You do?

Wait right there!

But...

In Bug Paradise, Yu'er listened closely to the first notes of the recital...

* *doubao*: also the name of a steamed bun stuffed with soybean paste (*dou*: soybean; *bao*: steamed bun)

Yu'er never saw the boy named Doubao
again. But one day, she found an old photo
of her grandpa from many years ago...

THE END

THE LETTER

It's so beautiful out today!

Huh?

Meow!

60

As time went by, I built up quite a collection.

Oh!

As fate would have it, I got one of the stamps in this series.

I had to find its partner.

One fine day, it showed up on a letter.

A-ha! Got you at last!

Now, if the addressee will just let me have it!

Fingers crossed...

Hello!

Uh...

A-are you Miss Gu Xiao'an?

And that's how the stamp found its partner. And a bit later, that lady and I were a couple too!

Because that lady...was your grandma, Yu'er!

Gramma?

Tell me more about Gramma, Grampa! Do you miss her?

I'm sad she's not around anymore. I have so many things to tell her!

Oh sure! She was a gem. She used to tease me all the time, but she had such a big heart.

That night Yu'er's grandpa had an incredible dream. He was a mailman again, and the people who lived along the hutong were lining up to post their letters.

Yu'er dreamed about her grandma too.
It was something pretty special…

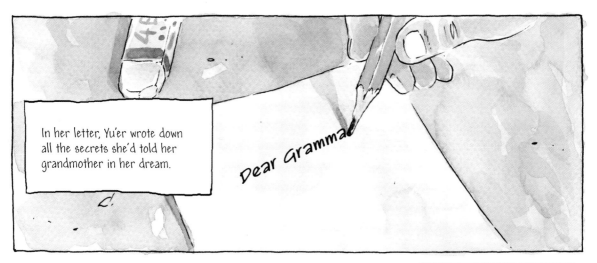

In her letter, Yu'er wrote down all the secrets she'd told her grandmother in her dream.

Although her grandma's old house had been demolished, her grandpa still remembered the address.

Yu'er's letter to her grandma vanished into the mailbox...

A-ha! Got you at last!

Now, if the addressee will just let me have it!

Fingers crossed...

Dear Gramma

My name is Yu'er. I'm your granddaughter! We sort of met already, in my dream. Grampa thinks about you all the time and misses you a lot. I hope you get this letter. We love you. Oh, also—the mailman who comes by your house is really sweet! Be nice to him! Hee hee!

Yu'er

THE END

KIDS AT HEART

Expressions in Beijing can be quite colorful. For instance, if someone's "rolling a train around his mouth"...

...it means he has a talent for talking.

Grandpa definitely had the gift of gab! A train brimming with stories ran all around his mouth.

One day, Yu'er asked her grandpa's friends if he ever got tired of talking.

Ha ha! Good one! Tell us another!

Young lady, you're hilarious.

Grandpa replied, "My stories are a balm for our little hutong. They ease the soul's little boo-boos."

Pumpkin Jr.! Dabao!

Yu'er! What story is your grandpa going to tell tonight?

* A sixteenth-century (Ming dynasty) novel by Wu Cheng'en, one of the four great classical novels of Chinese literature

Eh?

Why, it's ol' Pumpkin! Pumpkin, my pal!

113

Ol' Pumpkin's almost cute when he's painting.

In this little hutong, all the boys and girls have their own big dreams...no matter how old they really are.

THE END

A HUTONG SKETCHBOOK

Beijing is a city in the northern area of the People's Republic of China. It also serves as the country's capital. Beijing has one of the largest populations of any city across the world. It is home to more than 21,500,000 people. It has been China's capital during most points in Chinese history from 1297 onward. (The capital was elsewhere from 1368 to 1420 and from 1928 to 1949.) Both new buildings and older, more traditional spaces make up modern Beijing.

In *My Beijing*, Yu'er, her grandfather, and their neighbors live in an area known as a hutong. In a hutong, courtyard houses form a narrow lane or alleyway. The grounds of these houses have yards on the inside, beyond the houses' living spaces. Side by side, the homes' outer walls create the space of the hutong. Hutongs often join together to make larger neighborhoods.

Hutongs have been a part of Beijing's culture for hundreds of years. People began to create these spaces during China's Yuan dynasty (ca. 1271–1368). More hutongs appeared during the Ming (ca. 1368–1644) and Qing (ca. 1644–1912) dynasties. These neighborhoods capture both a traditional way of building homes and a traditional type of community. In more recent decades, many of Beijing's hutongs and surrounding homes were destroyed to create room for new buildings. However, other hutongs are treated as protected areas. They are also popular travel stops for visitors to Beijing.

ABOUT THE AUTHOR

Nie Jun was born in 1975 in Xining, in the province of Qinghai, China. He began drawing at an early age by copying *lianhuanhua* (traditional Chinese palm-sized picture books of sequential art). He soon became a fan of Osamu Tezuka, Zhang Leping, and black-and-white pirated editions of Tintin. As a teenager, he won a contest sponsored by a comics magazine and had his drawings published for the first time. Later, he was deeply influenced by the range of works within the Chinese comics scene, as well as by Japanese artists Akira Toriyama and Katsuhiro Otomo, not to mention Moebius (the French cartoonist Jean Giraud). In 1995 he began to publish his art in magazines. He lives in Beijing and teaches drawing to university students.